The Place Within

Carolyn L. Seymour

iUniverse, Inc.
New York Bloomington

The Place Within

iUniverse books may be ordered through booksellers or by contacting:

iUniverse
1663 Liberty Drive
Bloomington, IN 47403
www.iuniverse.com
1-800-Authors (1-800-288-4677)

Because of the dynamic nature of the Internet, any Web addresses or links contained in this book may have changed since publication and may no longer be valid. The views expressed in this work are solely those of the author and do not necessarily reflect the views of the publisher, and the publisher hereby disclaims any responsibility for them.

ISBN: 978-1-4401-3491-3 (sc)
ISBN: 978-1-4401-3492-0 (ebk)

Printed in the United States of America

iUniverse rev. date: 8/20/2009

Contents

HURT

Theft 2
Collegiate Suicide. 3
Storm. 4
Separation 5
Incarceration 6
The Day My Dad Went Away 8
Father of Faith 9
Missing 10

NEW THOUGHTS

Awakened 12
Perspective. 13
Gratitude. 14
Prompt: What do you believe is the biggest problem
    teens face today? 15
Renewing My Mind. 16
Couldn't I?. 17

ADULT

Your Wish is My Command. 20
Enticement 21
Life Addition 22
Self Discovery 23
Assessment. 25
Preparation 26
Harmony 27

FOOTPRINT

Generations 30
Focus. 32
The Last of Its Kind 33
March On 35

Picture You 36
Babes of the Ancient 37

ATTITUDE

Fala 40
Where I'm From 41
Dust Your Shoulders Off 42
Mine 44
It's like dis 46
Battle 47
You Forgot 48

JUST FOR YOU

New Love 50
Godmother 51
A New Father 52

HOPELESS

The End 54
Roadblock 55
Left Behind 56
Letting Go of Your Senses 58
Soldier 59
False Freedom 60
Last Days 61

THE #8

New Birth 64
Words 65
Make love to me 66
Truth before Armageddon 67
A New Beginning 68
Ensuing Exodus 70
22-Day of Light 71

LILLIES

Everywhere 74
Good News 76
Who Reads Poetry Anymore? 78
Fill 'er Up 79
It's Yours 80
Vision 82
Contagious 83
Like Air 84

WHEN I THOUGHT IT WAS LOVE

Convincing 86
Free 87
Oblivion 88
Healthy 89
Head Over 90
Lost You 91
Enough 92
To Grow and Love You for You 93
The Same Old Song 94

A DREAMER

Restless 96
Let Me Sleep 97
Nightmares 98
Fire 99
Where Did All My Lovers Go? 100

JUDGMENTAL

Love Poem for the Slain 102
Mixed 103
Street Corner 104
Dear Brother 105
Lead 106
Drug Dealers 107

HURT

Theft

Blue balls, blue streak, blue crew

Hey take this
I don't want it anymore
All I want is pure emotion and confusion

To be blind of my pitiful reality
That is not choosing my true identity
Embarking on your destruction
Demolishing the youth, my youth

Trade my life for a nickel
And spread my thighs; enter
And I shall perish and no wounds can heal
This great divide; so take this

You'd like it
No blue balls, lots of blue streaks
And your crew into me

Take my destiny
Rape my time and air for your indulgence
And joy under these lips and in between
No bitter cry
Pure emotion and confusion

You raped me

Collegiate Suicide

I forgot why I came here
I partied and drank
I'm tired of writing and walking
Everything is confusing and emptiness fills my throat
I puke and cry
My focus misguided to pitchers of alcoholic drinks
I do not speak my voice or my words
It is not I who am writing
I am not true to who I am
I am lying to you
And something chokes me up and my throat aches
I lie. I lie. I lie.

This is not me.
I am not writing these...
I am scared
I am dead to real life
I do not see reality
I don't see you or myself
God is a mystery to me
I lie to him too
I die. I die. I die.

I awaken and I am mystified
I am clueless
I am tired
I forgot why I came here
Reversing to the time I was fed through a chord
And am now only spirit
It wasn't my choice and I am gone
In and out of sight
Lonely, roaming the earth
And no one can hear or see me

Storm

The loveless life
Equivalent to a loveless storm
Cruel intentions headed your way
Wonder why you stay
And let them strike you down
Lightening, your frown
I see why your face torn
Beat and withered by the rainfalls down your face
Love doesn't seem like it can take rain's place
Rustling winds have you been in
Hair matted and clothes torn
I hear the mourn when the wind warns
Only a little light
In the darkest night
Seems like the same in your sight
Full of fright with no insight
I see you don't sleep tonight
But in the morn
You will mourn no more
For a loveless storm
Can't last forever
Remember the past tense of torn

Separation

You say my name is Value
Is that true?
Am I significant?
If that is so,
When I'm around her, it diminishes

Is it that she reminds me
Of those who belittled me
And tried to shove my mouth shut?

Is it because I am young
Becoming adult?
She treats me like a child
And expects me to act above what she calls me

Dumb ass, stupid, retarded motherfuck
If I have value
When she's around it diminishes

I cannot talk to her
No longer in fear of what she might say
But she doesn't care to understand
And doesn't hold her tongue
When I needed her most just to listen

How can I get her to talk to me
The way that is understanding?
But I think then
What's the bother?
Since I no longer have value
She made it all diminish

Since she came around, it all diminished

Incarceration

Oh that light
Breaking through my optic nerves
Into my hypothalamus
Into my mouth
Screaming through the cries

Bars and glass become temporary death certificates
Til my father comes back from his coffin
And my brother too

To die and you told the truth
To die and you told the lies

So biased the systems here, yesterday and today
That will be here tomorrow til my last

Oh that light
So precious, you see?
That night will fall and
Penetrates through screens, windows and cracks of the doors
A world too crazy to explore
Discourages the youth to move on

Oh that light
When it's stolen
It is like you'll never get it back
Co-extensive distressing emotions and
Unpleasant sensations
overwhelming the nerves and soul

That coffin will open
Three will step out of the filth and
Severe mental suffering
The bars and glass and coffin have caused

That light will have lavish intentions

To shine on us
Reflecting the light we always had
And the light no one wanted people to know

That's all right, that's all right
Bars and glass not as strong as light
It can't be destroyed
It can't be drained of its might

The Day My Dad Went Away

Although he has left many times before, at this time I was unable to see the severity of the situation. And I miss him due to his actions. And all year I still haven't seen him, but every night I pray that tomorrow will be a better and new day for me and my father. I wonder sometimes if the reason for his leaving was to learn of his mistakes, being prisoner to live with this knowledge and be away from his child – his children. Daily hoping that we will meet again in my house in my room in my heart so that where ever I go, my heart is healing because he is here. I wonder what life is like for my father and I wonder how he can take so much pain.

Father of Faith

Are you crazy? Why did you go? Even after so many letters and the years I had faith in you. Didn't that mean anything to you? And if it did, how come it isn't enough? You love me, right? You said you did. And everyday I wear the ring. Today, wondering if you're alive or dead.

How come? Why? And all those questions unanswered. Spoiled in your youth and it wasn't your fault – accidents happen. You don't have to live up to the curses put upon you. In some ways I feel like you've cursed me, but I rebuke it. The daughter does not have to take after you. Look at me. Look at what my mother, my family and my friends raised. I'm standing here. Don't see me? I look like you, with long hair and a big smile. Don't know me? Wasn't I yours? I thought I was; at least for 21 years.

It hurts so badly, but I know I can't do anything about it. I do have a father that loves me and I'll get to go home anytime I want to. And we talk everyday. And he watches over me and makes sure I'm fed. And I guess that's all that matters – even though you couldn't provide for me. My Father did and always will. Maybe one day you can try to follow His example.

Missing

It's funny how crazy you are
It's funny that you are not here
It's funny how gym shoes fade from my memory
Who gave them to me I wonder?
It's funny, so twisted
I know it's funny
I have laughed tears and cried happiness
People brag about theirs and I have nothing to say
I needed you, but there is no way you can save the day
It's so twisted it's funny
Where did you go?
Where did you stay?
You were to be here with me
But you were missing

NEW
THOUGHTS

Awakened

3 shades of blue and white
Eyes are lazy
And lessens my excited sight
Love the bright
Sun in my eyes
Tired eyes
Yet clearer, wise

Perspective

There are many things I write
Due to not knowing how to recite
All the wonders in my sight
Too beautiful, can't fight
I'm over 1,000's of feet above the clouds
And I could only glare at this wonder and say wow
All the metal and paper in the world
Can't amount to this
This innocence is such bliss
Wishing to kiss the clouds, hold them in my arms
But gravity demolishes my wish to demonstrate my charm
Love the world; hate the world I'm constantly sayin'
But who am I the one to be okayin'?

Gratitude

How dare you and I cry?
Cry, cry, why?!?
We are blessed
Rather than the rest of the world
Being forced down
And someone's digging in their chest

Cool waters
The thought makes my heart soar
And all roars can be brought to a close
No mistakes of foes can bother me.

Prompt: What do you believe is the biggest problem teens face today?

Figuring out who they are, what they believe in, and what they should be. We are all trying to find our place in the world and sometimes we can get lost without guidance.

Renewing My Mind

I'm tired of disappointment, recklessness and chaos that I can't find peace in because I've caused it. The devil tries so hard to bring me down with remembrances, feeling and actions of my past sins and now that I recognize this, I know that it only occurs because I permit it. My father has forgiven me – bottom line. I am made new and it is time that I think that way. How can I do God's will if I feel that I am not worthy? I am worthy, I am able, I am loved, I am forgiven, I am here, I am here! Carpe dieum for real this time around; for real this life around.

Blessed be.

Couldn't I?

Blood is what I want
For it represents so many things
Blood is my only request from this world
Be it warm or cold this is my only promised
This is my only thirst

If I could burn all the money
And melt the copper, nickel, gold, platinum
And everything of "value"
I could have satisfaction – couldn't I?

Dear illusions or Lucifer
Which ever you like
I want your blood
Your slain
Why do you still exist?
We feed you, I'm sure
But what if I put a stop to all of that

Your blood would not exist
And everything would be right in the universe

ADULT

Your Wish is My Command

Whisper something in my ear
Tell me what you want
Make my eyes close
I exhale at the thought
Tell me what you want and
I'll do it.

Whisper to me all of your desires
And take me to that place
Is this what you want?
Ice cubes on my lips
You tasting my hips
And stroking my every curve

My tongue on you
The pull, the stroke, the rub
Is this what you want?
To tug with your teeth
And suck with your lips

To enter this stream of ecstasy
And arrive all over me
I will be your desire
But you must tell me what you want

Love me
Whisper something in my ear.

Enticement

Why did I do it?
I didn't mean to breathe or listen
I walked normal
Didn't flaunt my curves and hair
I was me
And he wanted to caress
I said no like sixty times
And no we didn't "Do It"
But I touched his flesh
And my skin started to boil
How those sexy brown eyes
And soft smooth lips seem to
Capture me and control the urges from within
I am sorry my love
I swear I didn't mean to breathe or listen

Life Addition

Multiply Divide Add Subtract
In these thighs are multiply
In hers are divide
In us love is add
Without us is subtract

Tell me math that you like
Which one first
Which one last
Which one never

Be add and multiply

Love me math or are you science?
Now I am, Now I am
I am confused

You said science and I said math
I wasn't good in Biology
Nor Chemistry maybe Anatomy
Cuz I wanted to study you

Are they both, are they equal?

You be science and I'll be math
And we can Elevate.

Self Discovery

Him: Who are you?
I do not know your name
You've walked by 6 times
And I did not call your name

Her: Who am I?
Her Thoughts: I walk tall and hear this whisper
But I am afraid to grasp the words
Tip toe, tip toe
Leap, crawl
Go into this
Sweet legs, thighs, hips
Her: What is your name?
Blue green eyes
How do you move?
Do you linger?
Do you run?
Do you lie?
Do you yell?
Do you cry?
Who are you?
Why don't you speak?
Am I asking too many questions?
Did you hit?
Did you touch?
Who are you?

Him: I am tall, I am strong
I try honesty; I succeed mostly with others, but not myself.
I struggle, but it makes me try harder.
I love Him and we walk together to build me up higher.
I am contempt with you if you will have me.

Her: I am loved and I am yours.

Both: I am you

Her: Do you want fingertips?
            And titillating taste bites?
            You want to rub don't you?

Him: You want to sing don't you?

Her: Yes, lay here
            Come, lay inside

Both: Love be willing

Assessment

Black board, green board
Chalk erasers
Dry erase markers
And white board

Language me
And study me
Proceed with your formulas
And I'll exclaim my theories

Love me pencil
And love me pen
Time for F or A

Grade my tongue
And I'll grade your hands

Be my teacher
And I'll bring you Fuji

Taste that bittersweet
And I'll feed you my eyes and ears

Write me down on Tuesday
And I'll bring you the appointment

I'll be that inspiration
And you be that spontaneity

Bite into that apple
But don't bite off too much

I'll grade your hands
So be careful how you touch

Preparation

Love me for me

Love me for the hairs on my head, made for you to touch
Love my soft skin that I moisturize for you to caress
Love my ears because I decorate them for you
Love my breasts for I flaunt them in your direction
Love my pussy for it's only yours
Love my heart for it's imperfections, striving to be good for you
Love my lips only for your pressure
Love my voice, I sing for you and our love
Love my mind because without it I cannot walk to you
Love my spirit so that I may be with you when I die
Love God for he made me and you

Love me for me
I was made in his image and so were you

Harmony

Teach me this rhythm
This drumming and thumps of step
Move my feet in that glance
Show me the sway of your wrist
Let me follow

Teach me this rhythm
That style in you that grace
Take my fist and let my fingers separate
Show me this way of your kiss
Let me follow

Teach me this rhythm
This vibration and breath in you
Take my arms, make them limber
Show me the art of your grasp
Let me follow

Teach me this rhythm
That love you profess to me
Take my legs and let them spread
Show me this love of your path
Let me follow, let me follow
    Rhythm

FOOT
PRINT

Generations

Oh my God
The times are turnin'
Fire in these prying eyes
3rd degree burns
Body urns for the simple pleasure
Am I treasure
Am I woman?
Am I beautiful?
I died 50 years ago and 10,000 years ago
Though I was born or was I born 3 months ago
I wish I knew
Hell, I don't need to
All I need is to grow
Sow only precious seeds
Baby you can't give me what I need
And you are such a precious seed
This I know
I don't want you
I don't need you
I want to touch you
Tease you
I do love you
Why would I say what I said above?
Because I am no dove
I struggle with so much fire
Waitin' to make me die
Steadily and steadily I cry
And try not to cry
Get me out this world in peace
After all my talents have dried up like yeast
Knowing that I am a temporary beast
When I think of only me at the least
Don't matter if I go east, west, north or south
I will end up in the same place
Whether I'm living or covered with lace
Can't blame the dysfunction of my face and name

Hopefully when I leave
The world will never be the same

Focus

The seeds have been planted
Grown to the skies
My black people
Deep rooted and so wise
I have so much history
It surpasses the pain
Let us live on
Not die in vain

My black people
We struggled but we have prevailed
And all our inventions and discoveries
Much pride must be unveiled
So I say again
We shall remember always and trust
That our future only exists
Because of those who came before us

My black people
I love you and thank you
Let us not lose sight
Of what we are here to do

The Last of Its Kind

How do I begin when I am at my end?
I started at the finish line and my foot fell to ashes
And then I jumped away from the runners of the streets
I have never sunken to the sewage that consume feet of many
Mine went to ashes before it could grab the flesh
I want to eat fast and frequently to dry up my hands that had salt water
sprinkled over them
"Who did it?"
I ask to the crowd
"Who ate my precious cheese and crackers?"
It is all I have left after the salt water in my hands dries up
And my hands turn to ashes
I like the light and if it is the sun
I turn to ashes much quicker
And I can't run or hide under a tree
They were all cut down and burned last week
"Who did it, who took my oil?"
Oh I can't believe it
I have no fuel for my skyrider on my roof
I can't fly away
And now my arms turn to ashes
And I slide off the roof
"Who said I was on the roof? Who said I was on the roof? Who said
I was on the roof?"
I cried and it trickled to my left knee
And if felt like acid
Acid rain that took the forest and animals that could of cured cancer
Poor frogs I will miss you
Unless someone finds you and takes care of you soon
"Does anyone care?"
I slid off the roof and fell on my but-tocks
My legs caught site of the sun
And I roll over and try to hide
My hide turns to ashes
And my eyes roll and roll
I can't cry anymore

"Who did it? Who took tear ducts and said for my eyes to roll lonesome on the ground?"
How could you
I was the last one left
And I had no one to put my eyes in a jar to keep me safe from that supreme light in the sky
That made my flesh like ashes
Slowly my tissues fade and my pupils sink
There is nothing left to see
Get out of here
Let the remains be

March On

And everything was slow
Tears unwept or either frozen
Silence in the fallen snow
Covering the past
They found freedom at last
These dead bodies remaining
Not able to march on
Life was in thoughts and in the air
But death was the only promise
It gave freedom and no despair
Can such wounds of suffering be repaired?
These gazing eyes penetrating into us a death stare
This will remain in our hearts
Such fools we are to think we are smart
We avoid chances to prevent harmful things
So blindly we do this
We dance, we sing
Thank you Jesus for saving MY soul
So blessed to be far from crematories powered by the coal
Be advised those living in the flesh
Die off those psychopathic dreams of being
Remember and accept this always
Death is only the beginning
It is your chance to change the world

Do not die in vain

Picture You

Picture me children.

Long hair that's drenched in dark brown
Standing almost with features of a Mexicano
5'1" mulatto, awaiting her many fates
Nineteen, awaiting my patience

Be patient my family
Your blessings come
When you can handle them in humility
They come with struggle and much pain
Almost to the point of wanting to end your life or others

Wait. God comes in perfect tense and sense
Wait. Life will be there when it's supposed to

Don't expect anything but God
And that one day you will want to follow God
Discovering God is everything

Know this; death is good, but never force it
Know this; life is good, but never force it

Feed your mind
But be careful of the junk placed on your plate

Picture me children
I am you
Your brother, sister

Live – Love God. Die – Love God.

Babes of the Ancient

When talk is cheapened because no action followed
Broken promises leaving behind regrets
Little eyes with tears they wept
Let there be light and the promises kept
Forgot our roots and fears we beget
Come back
Where are my children
Bright eyes
Planting seeds for tomorrow
Just for the sheer delight of it
Lovers of milk, sweet
Easy to devour
Cold hearts
Empty ears
Their tongues they swallow
Everything regurgitated
I still must have hope
I am not the giver of life
Neither can I take it away
And if they go
If they stray
I must still stay awake every morning
Beating to my drum
Oh griot!
Telling the story of how it all begun
Thank you for your inspiration
O restless ones
My speech is deepened
Rolling off a steady tongue
Begin again and again
And again, again
The race ain't over yet
But the race is surely won
Hallelujah!
Glory be

ATTITUDE

Fala

Fala exclaimed the cat
Beautiful did she seem to gleam
Known for the extraordinary titles of dime piece and queen
Flossin' off the seams and she leave you screaming…
Volente! Volente! Merci
This cat is such a lady
You'll be quick to reflex after her orders of oostani
And her fragrant flesh will leave you breathless.
The C to the L to the S
Why should I speak of anything less?

Where I'm From

I am from the last day of preschool
Onto the rocks and asphalt
Onto the playground then
Onto the lawn
I am from those tall buildings
Crooked, cracked now demolished
I am from the crack heads and prostitutes
I am from my house sitting on a dead end
Running, running from it
Into a car to sleep
I am from many nations
And you ask me and I say hybrid
I am from many worlds
And you ask me and I say God
My spirit free to roam
And be imprisoned by body resting in what life can bring
I am from New York, Georgia, Washington, California, Tennessee,
Illinois, Louisiana, Virginia, Maryland, Virgin Islands and Ohio now
I was from Africa and then I penetrated other lands
I was from dust and now here I stand
And scream and shout
Ain't it pretty, ain't it funny
Ain't it sad, ain't it a blessing?
Ain't it me?
Flowing in and out of dimensions
And you see me
See my picture, my story, my fam
I will not fail

Dust Your Shoulders Off

I'm scared sometimes
Wishing to be blind
Or be at home with our Father
Because I see so much
That I'm scared of myself
Who am I to judge?
I'm dangerous
Being a fire starter
That they gon' hate so bad
Sometimes I can't stand this shit
I ain't perfect motherfucker
So you can lick my clit
I'm tired and lazy
Unmotivated and removed from existence
Realizing I can't see everything
I need to shut the fuck up and be humble
Dare I die?
Dare I stumble?
Sayin' I'm just too sweet
My cookie crumbles
Bitter taste rising through my eyes
Who am I scared of?
Fate, don't ask me why
Shouldn't be no pity here
Shit gettin' sticky
Should have left long ago
Who put me here?
Why? I say to air and smoke
Filth stays, sleeps, rises, surprises
Never realizes its imperfection
Til I smack it out of my way
Off my feet, off my mind and heart
Where should I go, where should I start?
Hopelessness wants me so bad
It's willing to drop its draws
And fuck all the fire outlaws

Lost, found, lost, found, lost, found
Can't make up my mind
Are we living to tell lies?
Or are we living to tell truth?
Demolishin' the youth
And our dreams fade
Cause confidence was delayed
Didn't nobody say we could do good
Didn't nobody say we could do bad
Didn't nobody say shit
They didn't say a got damn thing
What the fuck is going on?
Aren't we so beat and torn already?
Ain't we blessed, ain't we cursed
And that we have rehearsed
Whether of the inquiring minds
Or those trying to survive on the streets
Having gone to the limits
To drought, to flood and then back again
Devastation says, "Ha ha. It's just too easy to win."
Who gon' stand up?
Whose gon' grab dey nuts?
And grab dey tits?
And say fuck ya, fuck dis
Disaster can't dismiss me
Disaster ain't a friend of mine
Devastation has no place for inquiring minds
And survivors of the streets
Disaster is gon' beg for its life tonight
It's gon' scream at you, and you and you
"Get me the fuck out of here. Don't you hear me? I'm all you got. I'm
the only thing that's been there for you. Help me."
Fuck you, I say
Who's with me?
Scream if you down
Kiss my ass if you ain't
Disaster disappear
We layin' new paint

Mine

Folded and scraped and carved
Stolen, beaten and starved
Like that wood that could
Like that precious diamond that stood
Kind and merciless
Murderer and countless bliss
Time here
Time there
Time, time for you to stay
Time, time for you to scream
Time for you to realize that being
Yes, carved, beaten and folded
Yes, starved, scraped and stolen
It's golden and it sparkles too
It's blinding and it's crying for you
Yes it stood so firm so strong
Yes it was her but left for too long
Left for too long
Cry, laugh, scream, whisper
Die, live, awake, sleep
What don't we have in common?
I'm v'd out and you d'd out
Vagina, dick
Vagina, dick
Fuck you
You ain't the only one who can stick
Stick, I stick, I stick up for me
I stand, I rise, I rise, I rise
Don't confuse me with murderers
Don't confuse me with the damned
Spirit flies high, low, in between
No different, can't you see
Learn, die, wait
Wait, learn, die
Learn, wait, die
Yes, this is what I ask

Yes this is what I want
I pick the last combination
With the addition of change
Stuck between learning and death
That's my story I hope
That's my cry, laugh, scream, whisper
That's never to be denied

It's like dis

It's like dis
I just need to beat up myself
Wantin' to hurt every body
Wantin' nobody's help
Selfish with the time and verbal
Just tired of niggas
And my damn self givin' me trouble
Men of my past inspired me yesterday and today
Who am I to make decisions just to better my way

Selfish with the time and verbal
Ready to open myself
Ready to explore
Call me up
But you must call to teach
And to be knowledgeable
Don't trip off the scene
Don't be lost to the point you confusin' even me
Be lost to the point that you know about it when you find me
It equals Him the only it there should be
Not the Sh-it or the it-aly

Selfish with the time and verbal
It don't matter no more
You've demised the cry
Disguised the why
Deprived the sky
It's like dis
I will be apart of one and it
I'll fucking fly to Italy and you can't say shit

Battle

Quick like dust
Slow like fermented yeast
You stare so hard
Evolving into a monstrous beast
Oh poor you, staring, glaring so hard
Thinking dis my world, I'm the superstar
Why are you here oh triflin' awh
No mind paid to looks or words you think got me shook
Psychotic is the name for the games that you play
Watch closely 'cause I know you hear me
Close those doors, ain't nobody moving out
Go head, scream and run and shout
'Cause I know you need to
Nervousness got you shook
Ain't nobody gon' please you
Come on now, how you gon' act?
You was this monstrous beast
Before I laid down the map
See my destination, big star and all?
Baby we's big pimpin' and you about to fall
Tryin' to wreck my mood
But here you go now down at ya knees
"Lady/Pimp let me go. I'm begging you please."

Please, mercy left before I shut the doors
Crowd screamin' louder like
"We want some more!"

So you see how I spit
It's breakin' you down
Stand up 'cause I don't go for the crowd

Round 2 standin' on concrete
Should know I'm not the one to defeat
He nervous steppin' to the stage
Rappin his rap, but it ain't fillin' the page

You Forgot

I'll always look at you half eyed
If I look at you, I think I know what I will do
I'll smack you
But I long for your eyes on mine
But still I will crush you
Because you forgot I am a queen-royalty
Who belongs on the throne
Bring your voice down to a lower tone

JUST FOR YOU

New Love

I had an epiphany
I am breathing for the 2nd time
God gave me back the fated me
And you will share that breath with me in eternity

I was awakened from a cold and dungeon-dampened sleep
You have carried me out into the sunlight
To be warmed by it's luster and your heat

My mind has been replenished
Seeking knowledge, sharing my wisdom
You have ignited the vision in me

Now realizing my true nature
You have brought the best of me to the forefront
And dared me step across my boundary line

I indebt my soul to you
And share my spirit
Live inside of me
Be my valentine – forever mine

I had an epiphany
And it was you
A second breath
A destiny

Godmother

He is mine
If only for a little while
His sight, speech and walk
He will be tall and strong
Very intelligent, but never bold
He will give new meaning
To this dear life I hold
The very essence of my being
My vow to him to never cheat or be deceiving
I will try to erase the selfishness within my heart
This you will learn
We shall never part
To my godson
I vow to be there for you
If you shall ever need me
To my godson
I love you and this will always be

A New Father

It was crazy to think
That in a blink you'd be the one

Buying diapers and playing
Envisioning fun with your son

You are a grown ass man
And now I can clearly understand

Your life in the hands
Of the Almighty Father and friend

I am so proud of you
And what you are destined to see

With such determination
A star you will surely be

A leader taking it a day at a time
Working by faith; best believe… your life marked sublime

I'll remember always your love is true
And over the river with golden stalls
I will be seeing you

Not to be left behind or forgotten
Many enemies and haters over trodden

I love you and this new life
Will be full of pain and strife

However, your mind built for stamina through time
Remaining clear and balanced; never blind

Again, I love you and am so proud of you
Forever faithful, Lady C, eternally true

HOPELESS

Yet there is hope if you want it.

The End

One more time I see the light
I am bleeding to death
One more time I see your beautiful sight
I love you to death
One more time I see my hands
Torn and broken, aging to death
One more time I see the light
My body lays amongst the dead

Roadblock

I feel deprived of the determination to do better
Indulging into deadly things
People sky rocket
But I don't follow suit
In high pursuit of destruction
Close to reachin' demise
Define the word wise
And we won't define it well
For the wise they show you
But they never kiss and tell
Can't tell by the smell
Destiny is waitin' for you and me
Indulgin' in these deadly things
We shall die
Quickly or slow
Lost in rhymes
Seeping inside the flow

Left Behind

Breaking the glass in 6 in 16 in 22 in 45 in 300
Going mad and running into walls
Dirt laid on the ground
Long green stems and flower pedals
Mixed with blue yellow, white and blood
Cuts made into the heart of apexes
Open up to allow the passage to freedom
Dying air smothers the skin
And leaves room for sight
Encased in this solitude
Crushing the granules in the palms
And fingertips creating cherry paint
Transfer to walls and hair follicles
And a-lined dresses
Too proud to reach for lines and tones
Airy and light this three story told
And she falls
Deep into abyss

And troubles are left for those on the other end
Dirt laid on the ground
Long green stems and flower pedals
Mixed with salt water and despair

It was safe, but troubling
She said to come
I dove to meet her
And my legs were stiffened at the sight of truth
Noises and past lives
I plead for my escape
But there is no where
I will end up in the same place
Trusting eyes
I run to hide these thoughts
My escape, my prison, my journey
All grew and grew and realized

They'd all be one
One and no more, one and no more
Open eyes and see

Letting Go of Your Senses

Be gentle, go slow
Let this knife prick
And penetrate your skin

Blood scatters going down your cheek
Into your ear
And your hearing is clogged

Blow deep
And let the air leave your body
Relax and let it drip from your fingertips

Look at this ceiling
And wish you were not here
Walk. Haunt.

Soldier

He looked broken as his eyes seemed to gaze into the future and tears he fought because he saw a glance of the past. 'I feel restless' he thought. 'No matter how hard I try to stand, someone is always trying to sit me down'.

Hopelessness seemed the only possible fate and sometimes it is the easiest to accept. His hands were gray and rough as stone. His hair grew gray as to the ashes of a cigarette bud. It made me want to cry but only the sigh of understanding and the feeling that there is not much I can do was only expressed.

I gaze upon his flesh once more seeing the bones of his wrist and the cheekbones above the sunken areas on the sides of his face. I gazed into the corner of his eyes and I saw the whites of his eyes which had turned into the dead gray which seemed to consume his whole existence. I felt like I had stared through this fallen angel who had just lost hope for beauty; lost hope for the refreshing though of just being.

I knew that I could feel his spirit engulfing me as I tried harder to enter his world and at that moment I wanted to feel the skin that he was so used to. To walk around in it as if it were mine. His appearance redeemed my feelings from circumstances of the past. I remembered the thoughts of love.

He began to stand and his frown became loosened as awe scratched at my face. He stood and for a few moments he fixated his hands upon his hips. The confusion slowly lessened. His hands against his sides and militant he stood. Appearing strong, his eyes were calm and I breathed. Hope became a fog hovering over where we stood. I was across the road and he against a fence with grass lying out before the street and where the curb indented the earth.

I admired the flesh I saw before me and he walked away as if going to war contempt.

False Freedom

Deprived myself of such freedom
This bliss
Passionate minute spent on complaints and out cries
Considering all days spent searching lies
Found that they binged on my presence
Made blueprints to create by every tear

I held the pen and began to drown furthermore
Bringing crust and denial under my fingernails
No seed planted
Just time disturbed
Disturbed and lies lingered
Keeping oxygen away from my brain
No new world order to be maintained

Missing out on this peace
Deciding to stay numb
My kiss blended with crust and denial
That was seeded in my womb
The birth will give death and no answers
I stand and show my hands
And open my mouth to her
And she will cry
And I will be numb
This honesty will come
And my only explanation
For I was born and death is my only freedom

Last Days

And everything is like this
Some glued to a television
Others glued to space and hope for clean food and water
This is my family
I am trying to understand it
The minds of the greats would shine
There is too much blocking the light

And everything is like this
Nothing fast, nothing slow
Slaves to boxes and other electronics
Slaves to the systems that keep you hungry for justice

This is my family
And I am still searching for understanding
Wondering of when the days will come when poetry no longer tells
the truth
And black ink only left for representation

And everything is like this
Not much that I can do

THE #8

New Birth

Tasting the sodium chloride
Feet meshed in soot beneath the water
I crawl with cuts and gashes
A blackened eye

I clear these throats
Rising to fall
I am drawn in and out
In and out
Constant disruption
Chipping off the paint of hope

I'll knock you back to consciousness
And reseal these wounds
Wake up child there is no time to sleep

Cries and thumps from the ground
Released from my abdomen
Stagnant and loss of blood am I
A gash so deep
Still coughing
Must speak
My salvation and condemnation

The truth is not born
Instead it is ripped out
And thrown upon the dry sand

We crawl together
In and out of hope
Hoping to wake up and walk

Words

Lots of words, lots of time
Wasted, wrong words
Wasted with lies
Dear pen
Dear paper
You still don't seem to help get the message through
Does the paper rearrange the ink
Or do my words not yield inspiration
We torture, we cheat, we steal
Is there nothing better to do than just keep it real
Give it to me, give it to me now
I can't taste
I can hear that sweet sound
Sounds like heaven
Sounds like honesty, forgiveness and love above all else
Satisfaction is what I want
Reality is what I need
Just sit there, look and die
Die off the old ways
You know the ones
The ones where every body dies
We tries
We tries to change
Close it up
Steer hard
Not too far within our range

Make love to me

Make love to me
I want it here and now
Didn't have it before
Wasn't no where to be found

Make love to me
Why must I wait?
Why must I make excuses to further delay?

Didn't have it before
Wasn't no where to be found
Lost in the dark
Darkness just so full of sound

Make love to me
I want it here and now
I've denied me once again
That's something hard to forgive

But I didn't have forgiveness before
Wasn't no where to be found
Oh Creator, give love to me
I want it here and now

Truth before Armageddon

Call her goddess.

This girl
You know of her upside, not thru
She spoke to you twice
But her wind only tickled your toe
She had mild lovely expressions
Kissing of her speech
And she kept you tongue-tied

Blue streaks representing truth
Pouring down her leg
Running with tears and T-cells

Likely to be found thinking
The breath she breathes is angel-like and free of mind
She knows this...
This uncanny kind of love
Wants those sentences on your brain to love her family
And breathe like it's only for God and not shine

She knows tomorrow
You wish to borrow this knowledge
And something of a peace

Here
Release that ugh, that grime
And keep that brillo pad in the plastic
She knows it ain't over yet

Follow her

A New Beginning

Thank you for standing by
Listening and watching
Even when I shamed myself
You still rooted for me
And were rooted for me
Glory be!
I know we have an imperfect past
But we are still trying to shine
Fell short cuz we said that
The glory was "mine"
We meant the best
Had good intentions,
But forgot to confess,
Forgot to mention
We just kept repeating
Sounded like a scratched, broken, recorded, dust on it
Forgot to care for our voice
Shut ourselves up and out of the providence
We had so much in our hands
But just didn't know it
It's okay, it's okay now
Trust me, believe me
I'm here now, I'm here
I open my hands,
Since I can't hear you speak
I open my mind,
Since I don't know your history – yet anyways
I open my mouth,
Since you didn't say
I'm open, I'm open for business
Don't worry, I'll manage this well
I promise!
I don't want my pay docked
We'll have a new name for ourselves
It won't be the first
And most certainly won't be the last!

The family business is safe with me
Trust me, I'm here now
Believe in me
We are finally mindful and speaking
We are finally free

~ To my ancestors

Ensuing Exodus

I miss you poetry, my love
You used to ignite so much fire
And passion in my phalanges
And I'd write on envelopes and the backs of seats

And need you now more than anything
Spare my flesh and write my spirit
I miss you like the separation
Between God and I

Black death and vile melancholy kisses
And the breath of freestyle
Wanting to break out from
The vile lover's lips

I miss your burning fire
And long for your company
Feed my spirit
And make those tendons spell out my convulsions

Color me black and blue
The dark beauty full truth
And I will scream out many blessings
Elude the sickness of the mind
And sneak in healing of those wonder-us souls

Ignite me, unveil me
So to make the road ablaze
Breathe passion
Breathe you!
You can make me see your vision clearly

Wring eyes to take the morning crust out
There, better becoming already
Continuing the struggle with a new line of gasoline
Breathing to make it grow

22-Day of Light

The world can't bring me joy
And no man can bring me happiness
The man brings only a parallel continuum of the joy I share in Christ
Yes, my joy, my happiness is in you God

The world is not the foundation of trust
And no man can be trusted not even myself
The man shall trust in the Lord for my sake and I trust in the Lord for
his
Yes, my foundation is trusting in the Lord

The world can't bring me peace that surpasses my understanding
The man is also a soldier on God's battlefield
He watches my back and I watch his by praying to you O Lord
Yes, you are my peace in the midst of spiritual warfare

The world can't bring me love
The man can't give it to me either
He can only walk with me, I lean on him, he leans on me, but we are
both carried by God
Yes, you are my one and only love and in you I have love for myself
and the man

Yes Lord Jesus you died for me and gave me life
And in this life I have joy, trust, peace, love and now wisdom
Bring me the people who will walk with me
Parallel, looking to you for complete satisfaction – not me
We need you because the truth of this matter, dust, elements
We cannot co-exist without you

Keep my mind stayed on you

LILLIES

Everywhere

That's that love
Like when you go outside, it goes through, it makes things grow

That's that love
Like when you're done fighting and you get to breathe

That's that love
When you don't know what to say and they hug you anyway

That's that love
Coming from the winter into the spring you sing

That's that love
Quick and easy; slow and hard

That's that love
When no one's home and you become this superstar

That's that love
Brick layered and cemented and thoughts never demented

That's that love
So blue and wide; blanket to the brown and green

That's that love
When you die and you sing

That's that love
Crucial and brutal no matter how hard it be
You don't ever be alone even when you think, see?

That's that love
Powerful and mysterious
Makes me not want to be so curious

That's that love

Never destroyed, never repaired
Never blinding or lying

It's just there
Where's this?
Everywhere

Good News

And I adore
I adore you more than life itself
Imagine, breath is something I hold dear
But rather leave it and come into you
There is peace of mind when this is recited
And all stress begins its digression.

I'm under the impression
That all the world's a stage
But I defy it 'til my last page
We are more than actors
We actually feel
And contrary to our hypocrite roots
We still have the privilege to heal
There is peace of mind when love is recited
And all stress begins its digression

I'm under the impression,
That every vessel is meant to be destroyed
I claim it null and void
We all have the ability to be free
More than the ideals of Ms. Lady Liberty
And she been raping me for years
Waiting to catch a glimpse of prosperity
Due to my ancestry
But there is peace of mind when destiny is recited
And all stress begins its digression

I'm under the impression
That my body wasn't meant for me
I strike it down knowing I'm the Queen, see?
Sold into bondage and we claimed to be one flesh
Across cultures and levels of eloquent-ness
Are we nothing more than our wombs
And the breast milk from our chests?
But there is peace of mind when gospel is recited

And all stress begins its digression

I'm under the impression
That nobody knows who they are
Wondering why the day is so long
And yet they still cannot get far
Beyond galaxies and beyond our sunny star
He stands waiting to hold you eternally in his arms

There lies peace of mind

Who Reads Poetry Anymore?

Who reads poetry anymore?
I write it only in friction or revolving spots
Hoping to reach and inspire to grow
Lots of blood and tears in the words I sow

Who reads poetry anymore?
3,000 years of black poetry
Psalms, Proverbs, Revelations
I still skip to the beat of my hearts' sensations

Who reads poetry anymore?
Little me, my little world
Peace in heart, crazy in mind
Hoping the world ain't forever blind

Who reads poetry anymore?
Those hopes in eyes in words you see
Are you reading close?
Can you hear me breathe?
Like a song written to a beautiful melody
No order
Just love
Breathe . . . poetry

I still love thee

Fill 'er Up

I was never perfect. Imagine. I've made many mistakes and some that I would love to delete from my memory and those of whom I've hurt. Reality sets in knowing that I did fall. How could I know what it's like to truly want to live? And there is a hole that sits inside of us; beneath our bellies. We try to fill it with food, but that only puts more weight on it. We try to fill it with sex, but that leaves us feeling empty. We try to burn it with liquor, but we only throw it up. A hole cannot be filled with anything palpable. Do you want it? That is question? I mean, do you really want it? Are you scared and if so, what are you fearful of?

Don't you want your whole filled? And by whole, I mean your entirety. It's a beautiful thing. You get euphoria just thinking about this calm, this peace, and your insides are not shaken. It's like your standing still and everything else around us, including your flesh is moving. It's like, it's like you are in another world – stuck in samsara, but your spirit in nirvana. Well, at least til somebody doesn't know just who you are and tries to shake your spirit. The beautiful thing about this, is you don't worry about anything that is moving around you – it'll pass by soon. And I love you. Some people can't even say that because it's real hollow beneath – like the belly of the beast.

But you'll come. You'll come eventually...

It's Yours

The way I desire to write
Even as a little child I screamed poetry
Wanting to tell fibs and stories
Told many half truths with my pen and paper
Told many lies aloud
My writing has its own sound

When I was four, I began to write
They were funny little short poetries
At seven I wrote my first story
It was all a lie as my pen pierced the paper
Free to scream it aloud
Waiting to revise it if it didn't have its exquisite sound

A learned expression
I learned to love to write
When I saw a pen I had to have some paper
The swaying back and forth from poetry to story
But my favorite was poetry
I would listen to it as I read it aloud
I was always intrigued by its peculiar sound

Crying, wanting to scream but I write
Heaven equivalent to pen and paper
Epic less than my story
Life was and is my poetry
Hear I speak truth this time
Not afraid to say it aloud
Oooo don't you like that sound

Prying in my business I disguised it in poetry
Sing like you proud and sing it aloud
Don't be afraid to have your own sound
All you need is the thought to write
Then you need the pen and paper
Create your story

My chapter will soon close with no sound
Scream, cry and spit the story
Life such sweet sorrow such sweet poetry
Get it down to the science to write
He will provide you with the pen and paper
Last chance, last life, one time
Bleed it aloud

Vision

Rising of the setting sun
I know you to be glorious, breathtaking and warm
You warm my face and delight my heart
Allowing ease to set in my mind
Not perishing, but rejuvenated

I love you even when I see you not
Arise to meet me, arise that I may sleep – I love you still
For the sun does not rise and set on me
It continuously glorifies God, burning all around
Too beautiful for my eyes to have all the day long

I appreciate what you have given me
Yes, I am contempt with what I have
You made things so precious, when you only have a taste
I thank you for not giving us all
Thank you for not spoiling us rotten

Placing sight in my mind, covered my heart
Seen and not seen, but always beaming bright
And I await you for when I reach the other side
I can be spoiled then
How I wait diligently for that day

The rising of the setting sun
My life only a reflection of what, since time, has already begun
A world ever turning, waiting to be seen
Dull my senses to keep from perishing
And make my spirit more the keen

I wait for you – not idle
I wait for you – be it my darkness, be it my light
For you are constantly and generations from now
Gloriously shining in my sight

Inspired by Proverbs 29:18 and the setting sun

Contagious

Ahhchoo. Excuse me.
God Bless You.
Thanks. Ahhchoo. Sorry.
God Bless You. It seems like everyone is getting sick around this early
October.
Yeah, and it's a pain. Good day to you. Hope you don't get sick as
well.
Thanks. Good-ahhchoo-bye.
God Bless You.

Like Air

Yeah it was nice the way his hair flicked on and off his forehead
My cool hair dancing on the breeze and around my face almost tickling
my eye
Slowing our walk towards each other and to my surprise he said hi
Stepping, stepping closer almost bumping our heads

Yeah it was nice the way his eyes were perfectly indented
My cool lips, glossy and smooth, tried to reply
Slowing my breath so I'd gain courage and stop being so shy
"Hello, nice to meet you" and I truly meant it

Yeah it was nice the way his legs seemed to glide
My cool was everywhere, except in its place
Slowing the intensity of how we first met
Stepping into time that together would be a spectacular ride
The challenges I have now are not so hard to face
Love was glorious and our wedding date was set

WHEN I
THOUGHT IT
WAS LOVE

Convincing

All I am right now
I can only be accepted
For the curls in my hair
And the clothes that I wear
Don't stare at me
Cause see we are you and me
Don't judge me
Just let me be
Or love me for me
Darling, let me know if our love will grow
Into somethin' that they don't know is blessed
Baby, let's forget the rest

Free

I'm sorry I left many words unspoken
Never love symbolized with a token
So left with a heart that is broken
All because your words not spoken

Seeing this sky
Makes me want to flee
Far into the sea
You ask me why
Due to my cry
Which my ears have not heard
Mind says all words are absurd

I was told
To be bold
From the inner me
Which is why I must flee
Cause all these niggas
Won't stay away from me

Wish you could see
But only the ears of my unconditional
Can make my happy real
To wipe away many fallen tears
To encompass me and never fear
To indulge on his heart
And binge on his love
I'll know him from my God above

Oblivion

Why, why?
All in my eyes
But no cries
No flurries above, below
Intervening my mother womb
Takin' place so in my face
Through me, in me
Short of breath
So easy to rest
He's in my best

Healthy

Substances, Materials, and Elements
Through your skin and integumentary system
You sustain the harmfulness of the three I've addressed
Ashy eyes - dry and soft to the touch
Rubber skin and rubber tongue there to taste
Breath of alcohol and cigarettes
Mouth tastes of rubber, rum and ash tray
Blinding you of my truest secrets
Feelin' you from afar is all that I'm keeping
Stare and stare hard
I will disappear if you blink
The blink is death because you were tired of me
Are you tired of I and bliss?
Stare and tell lies
Stare and tell truth
Who will you speak truth to?
Is it I, you monster in disguise?
You are a prize after I win the super lotto
You are my motto that I wish to follow
But are you healthy?

Head Over

Your love inspires me
To be that lady pimp with confidentiality
Sometimes I feel your eyes searching for me
Miles away across many rivers and streams
I do the same and try to hold back to keep my desires tamed
I leave you unnamed just in case someone brings this to fame
I want to keep you precious keep you pure
Regardless of the world and what you and I will endure
Go on tour be the man you need to be
And remember that I will never forget thee
You'll be apart of my new heart and inner light
And never will I mistake you for something dirty in sight
Don't want to bring you strife and added stresses
And know, I don't love money and don't care about designer dresses
God is who covers me
Be in that grace with me and never flee from the light we have
Never judge us from our past
I want us to ever last
The many facets of the world
You be my man, I'll be your girl
Twirl and twirk it
I want to work it
Reminding you it's all worth it
Cause I'm that value
Mandatory to stay close to you
Never have to boast to you
You understand my needs
My divine qualities
So you see that I need you in my life
Yeah, you dat dime sight
Flesh is not what I seek
But your inner heart that's meek
That teaches me
Caressing me stressing me to shine
You represent my divine
Now baby be mine

Lost You

I lost you
Where did you go?
Hoping the love was true

What did you do?
Three windows cracked and one to blow
I lost you

Why did you leave?
On wrist bleeding, I need a needle to sow
Hoping the love was true

Why couldn't you stay?
Broken arrow aimed at my heart, no use of the bow
I lost you

Haven't I died enough?
Tears parked on the curb, no one helped to tow
Hoping the love was true

Did you love me?
Weeds in my grassy life, my broken mow
I lost you

Death between us now and forever
I am no longer like a sista, you no longer my bro
I lost you
Hoping the love was true

Enough

I drop my pen
And I walk away
Look at this
Hurt, pain, dismay
So treacherous
And where were you
You strayed
Take two steps
And you will no longer breathe
I warned you two times
And now I leave

Yeah you scream
You holla
You cry
There is no answer
You constantly ask me why
Come close, lay here, die

Twice I have loved you
Twice I have died

You took it and ran
No price to place
The love in my heart erased
Here is that cold shoulder
I see you
And know I've grown older

Take this hour, year, infinity
You might find that wisdom you seek
But now you knowing
Only blessings for the meek
No more turning the other cheek

To Grow and Love You for You

And I was trying to find myself after I abandoned all that I held dear
I became a slave to false feelings of love and affection
And when truth threw up all over my shirt
I didn't have a change of clothes or laundry detergent
I was naked, cold, and no one could help me
So I walked for 13 days confused, 10 days hurt
And 15 days to find some clothes again to hide
I was free of the old comfort of heartache
But my spirit was shattered for six months
I asked for forgiveness and began my healing
Although it still hurts sometimes
Once you're careless no one else gives a fuck either
So who is holding you up?
And who is holding you down?
Baby girl don't frown
Learn to stand your ground

The Same Old Song

He wags his tail and when I leave he barks for me to come back
His beautiful brown eyes made me want to keep him around for a little
while
But he was tied to a chain due to his nature and I showed him no
mercy
Terrible, but he had broken my heart three times before
So I quickly walk to my door to keep the past behind me
I move on

A DREAMER

Restless

I lay and yearn for a soft presence on my back
tender and embracing to the touch
But day after day my hunger for the company
upon my back lessens and my back is tense
like I forgot how to relax
and yet at times I know it all too well
Why?
My stomach tosses and turns
from my tea and peanut butter crackers

11:56 at night_

Let Me Sleep

What do I write?
Laying beside the candlelight?
Oh _____ how I am missing you
Always curious of your time and place
While time stares me in the face
'til I contemplate
Think of my mistakes
And learn from my past
This small breath of innocence; will it last?
I wonder, but the world's a thunder
Full of lightening waiting to strike
Why should I fight?
Hoping my future is bright
And I maintain my insight
Lord please let me sleep tonight

Nightmares

The clouds cover me in the mist
The miss of the tree miss its cut
Help me, running in time
Not a dime to trouble the crime
Make the sea wash me up
I up in air not on ground
No sound, but in a cloud
The clouds cover me in the mist
The miss of the tree miss its cut
Drifting, my love, help me, I'm saved
I miss you now, who is to blame?
Making the cut I trouble the same
I blister, but mister
I'm up in air not on ground
No sound, but in a cloud
The clouds cover me in the mist
The miss of the tree miss its cut

I wake up and no one there to help me
I'm saved, but never trouble me again

Fire

It is in me to write
This fire that relinquishes my fears
And distinguished the water that flows within
I am wishing to desire nothing but God
And I find myself in a dilemma
God is everything raw and living
To be loved, why do I need flesh?
Why not only spirit?
Why do I desire to eat of the flesh?
Walk amongst it and drown in it
I die awaiting this answer
Every second of step, flesh decays
I will rot and no one remember my name?
But Him/Her/It
My only satisfaction
My only thirst
That fire won't die down
I try flour and it roars
And my many angels try to put it out
It grasps hold to my fingertips and pulls me in
I am consumed by these eyes
This breath
That stance
Beauty and Beast
A bite and a kiss
I die waiting
I die in vain?

Where Did All My Lovers Go?

I watched them walk off
They stumbled along the way
But acted like it didn't happen

I watched them get on the plane
It crashed
And I never saw them again

I watched them swim into the ocean
And the jaws of it crushed their skulls
But there was no blood

Where did all my lovers go?
And they forgot to say goodbye
But by then they became non-existent

Did they think no one would notice?
I noticed and I prayed for them
Even when they made mistakes

I laughed when I tripped
I hugged and kissed them goodbye
I swam close to the shore

Was I wrong to do what felt good to me?

And did it feel good, honey
And I loved just letting out those long deep breaths
I was free, finally…

But where have all my lovers gone?

JUDGMENTAL

Love Poem for the Slain

Pain teach me to stop
Not stop growing
Growing like tall trees
Strong oak aroma and almost piercing to the touch bark
Diamonds in the soil and
My people are slain and
Tortured and starved
Why this agony?
We are all to blame
Especially my black community
Cut off my arms, feet, ear and nose
And you will still be able to see the truth
Touch it, smell it and hear it
Please run with it to tell the others
Others wish to stay blind to love poems
This is a love poem
Voicing my love for my people's suffering
Build me up; tear me down
I will still be here like the dust
And be like the diamonds you tried to steal
You said it was yours cause you found it
And you said it was worth more than 20 lives
What a surprise
Died two days before you spoke that lie
And where will you go to see the light?
Is it the sun, the diamond, our God?
Yes he's real
I am real
You are real
How can you steal?
When it wasn't yours to have
And punish others with?
I will be tall and oak scented and dangerous to the touch
Pain, teach me to suffer

Mixed

Where we come from, we ask them
But why?
We're all moving the same
Whose to blame why they ask these questions
17th century ignorance
And biblical pastime Cain and Abel

Weren't we brothers once?
Didn't we come from the same mother and father?
Okay, alright, I realize we messed up
But how long is it lawful to keep excuses
They should make expiration dates on excuses
Or should they?
Am I being too judgmental because I have seen the truth?

I was there once…
Destructed and destructive
Maybe I should be less critical
Be diligent and patient
Keep saying what I know is truth

We were brothers once
Same mother and father
Can we at least begin there?
Come on, we have the same bloodline
And even if you don't agree orally
I know you know me

Can we at least begin there?

Street Corner

With summer
All that jive talkin' seems to get worse
The more ignorant they sound
The more I start to believe the world can't get no better
Each spoken word reveals their mind is being wasted
My knowledge wanted to be tasted
But what's the point
Countless days spent smokin' joints
Never he I want
So badly trying to be heard of his absurd
What was said all true word
Cause I've seen with my ears
The blood, the pain, the tears
And never will I fear
But oh dear
Will they ever hear?

Dear Brother

Dear brother of mine, watching you tryin' to maintain your image of deadly fine
Hearing the roaring of your anger; the lost time you've whined
When will you realize the truth of this world?
Truthfully see what I see when I look outside those windows and look out at the stars
Smell what I smell when I ride pass a bar, car or superstar
We get lost in the world just by sitting down watching a box
We see all the things that are not real and supposedly entertainment
Everything imitation mixed with worldly imaginations
When will you understand the process?
Just simply understand why things are the way they are
Why we have bars, cars and superstars
Why you love to look fashionable with physique and fly gear
Why you steadily cuss and waste the very thing you use to contemplate
When will you understand your fate, dear brother, before it is too late?
When will you cry for someone other than yourself?
When will you feel what I'm saying to you other than the lyrics of songs you are constantly playing?
When will you see that you were beautiful before the age you tried to reprocess your mind?
Made yourself think that you're bad and who don't take nothing from nobody
Smiles in your face while he wants to be with your girl
Will you ever be who I once knew and come back to our Father?
Or will you ride deeper and fall farther and farther?
How long will you last dear brother of mine?
Before he slits your lips and makes that day your time
When will you realize I won't be here forever?
I can't protect you
I can't give you money, I can't make you something to eat, I wont' see you in the bed sleep in the morning, I can't say what's up with you, I won't …be
Dear brother when will you open your eyes to realize that you can't even see?

Lead

Inspiration some times leaves this world. My wishes is to place it in my hand to the pen and let the pen penetrate the paper, and eyes and ears. Love or Hate? The choice we struggle with daily. Not all our buttons have been pushed. Severest pover-tist have not committed to suicide bombings and theft. Who is pushing these buttons in the flesh? Ask your leaders.

Those who have power can choose the hate in order to destroy. Love they refuse to share, but they keep plenty for themselves; putting love for others on the shelf. Depressing inspiration, abusing it and under our noses keeping it in a corner to rot and wither away.

Leaders take full and careful measures; take full responsibility. Leaders, watch out for temptation to know the mysteries. Watch out for the righteous and free; they will be your fall. If you just stop, listen to the call of us all, you will suffer less. We will be content, but sometimes leaders forget that they are heaven sent.

God, let the wise desire to give of their wisdom. God, let those who don't desire wisdom, crave it and yearn for it like they miss their legs lost in crashes. Let us be dust to dust and ashes to ashes when our tasks have been completed. Leaders, take heed, you must know that you are needed. My people stand up for righteousness and uphold the laws of the land. Integrity. Respect. Honesty. Honor. Forgiveness. Thankfulness. Forever love above all. God please keep us. Never let your grip loosen or be destroyed.

Drug Dealers

You disgust me
Your many side effects
Big money makers
Capitalizing on death and ignorance
And if we were in our right minds
We might actually speak out about it
But the people perish for lack of knowledge
And if they have knowledge
They don't have the wisdom of applying it
Yes, you are despicable
And in turn
Because we say nothing
So are we
My dear government
In cahoots with pharmaceutical companies
Street and main stream